FOAL

This book is a work of fiction. Any references to historical events, real people, or real places are used fictitiously. Other names, characters, places, and events are products of the author's imagination, and any resemblance to actual events or places or persons, living or dead, is entirely coincidental.

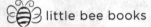 little bee books

An imprint of Bonnier Publishing USA
251 Park Avenue South, New York, NY 10010
Copyright © 2018 by Bonnier Publishing USA
All rights reserved, including the right of reproduction in whole or in part in any form. Little Bee Books is a trademark of Bonnier Publishing USA, and associated colophon is a trademark of Bonnier Publishing USA.

Library of Congress Cataloging-in-Publication Data
Names: Kent, Jaden, author. | Bodnaruk, Iryna, illustrator.
Title: The worst pet / by Jaden Kent; illustrated by Iryna Bodnaruk.
Description: First edition. | New York, NY: Little Bee Books, [2018].
Series: Ella and Owen; #8 | Summary: Dragon twins Ella and Owen ask their unicorn friends to help control the mischievous gremlins their parents bought them as pets—and the many gremlins that arrive soon after.
Identifiers: LCCN 2017055709 | Subjects: | CYAC: Dragons—Fiction.
| Brothers and sisters—Fiction. | Twins—Fiction. | Monsters—Fiction.
| Unicorns—Fiction. | Magic—Fiction. | Humorous stories.
BISAC: JUVENILE FICTION / Animals /Mythical. | JUVENILE FICTION
/ Humorous Stories. | JUVENILE FICTION / Action & Adventure / General.
Classification: LCC PZ7.1.K509 Wor 2018 | DDC [Fic]—dc23
LC record available at https://lccn.loc.gov/2017055709

Printed in China TPL 0318
ISBN 978-1-4998-0613-7 (hc)
First Edition 10 9 8 7 6 5 4 3 2 1
ISBN 978-1-4998-0612-0 (pb)
First Edition 10 9 8 7 6 5 4 3 2 1

littlebeebooks.com
bonnierpublishingusa.com

ELLA AND OWEN

THE WORST PET

by
Jaden Kent

little bee books

illustrated by
Iryna Bodnaruk

TABLE OF CONTENTS

1: SURPRISE? 1

2: A SQUEAKY NIGHTMARE 15

3: THE GOOFY GREMLINS 25

4: OWEN'S AWESOME GREMLIN TRAP!... 43

5: TWO UNICORNS ARE BETTER
THAN ONE 59

6: THE QUIET OF DOOOOOM! 69

7: THE MANE EVENT 77

8: BOOK REPORT 87

"I can't believe I met a unicorn—no, TWO unicorns!" Owen twirled about excitedly in the air as he flew with his twin sister. They passed the Gumdrop Volcano, flew over the Lake of Doom, and through the Valley of Things We Don't Want to Know About. They were on their way home.

"Well, I—" Ella began.

"And they gave me a ride!" Owen could barely contain his joy.

"That was—" Ella started.

"I already miss Sparkle Pop and Glitter Star so much," Owen said with a sigh. "Don't you? They are the best unicorns with the best unicorn names ever, right? They're so . . . so . . . unicorny!"

"I liked—" Ella tried again.

"And the riding!" Owen said. "Did I mention I loved riding a unicorn?"

"More than once. You know, I—wait!" Ella stopped and sniffed the air. "Do you smell that?"

"Oh! Is it a unicorn?!" Owen's eyes lit up.

"Of course not," Ella said. "Smell for yourself."

Owen took a big sniff. "I know that smell! That's bat squid covered in onions, acorns, and snail slime."

"DINNER!" Owen and Ella shouted at the same time.

The two dragons flew over one last hill and past the last tree in the forest before their home. They could see their family's home close by. They landed just outside of it, and Ella cried out, "Mom! Dad!"

Their parents, Daryl and Goldenrod, flew out from the house toward their children, nervously looking back over their wings.

"Owen! Ella! You're home!" their mom said.

"And not a minute too soon!" their dad added. "I'm still waiting for the stinky fish cake you promised me."

Owen shuffled his toe claws in the ground. "Yeah, about that . . ." he started to say.

"Oh, never mind," their dad said. "Your mom's made a lovely bat squid dinner with a fresh loaf of sourdough bread stuffed with raven's feet."

"We could smell it from over the hill," Owen said. "Delicious!"

"We also have another surprise for you," their mom added.

"Is it a jar of scale-cleansing bubble bath?" Ella asked.

"A new cushion for my reading chair?" Owen asked.

"Um . . . better," their mom replied.

"We wanted to surprise you both with . . . *pets*," their dad announced.

"PETS?!" Owen exclaimed.

"Are they snaggletoothed fire goats?" Ella smacked her tail against the ground like she always did when she was excited.

"Or are they sidewinder rattlebugs?" Owen asked.

"I think the best thing to do would be—" their mom said, looking nervously at their dad.

"To show you," he finished.

Ella and Owen quickly followed their parents into the house.

SMASH!

Plates and cups flew through the air.

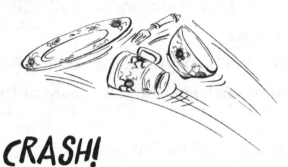

CRASH!

The kitchen table had been thrown on its side.

BASH!

Two small gremlins sat on a broken chair in the kitchen. Some pieces of the chair had crumbled to the floor. One gremlin was bashing pots and pans together while the other ate a large candle like it was corn on the cob. Broken dishes were scattered across the kitchen floor.

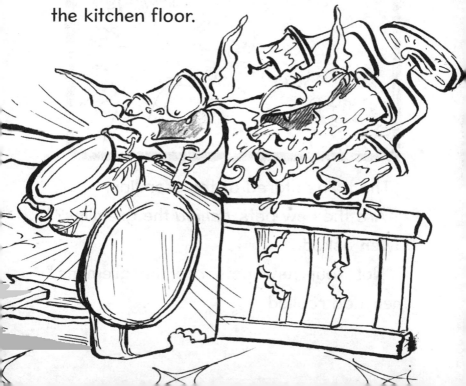

The gremlins had short, thin arms and legs, large noses, and potbellies. They had pointy ears that perked up when they saw Ella and Owen.

"And . . . well . . . here they are," Ella and Owen's dad said, cracking a weak smile.

The twins stared at the gremlins.

"Are the new pets *behind* the gremlins?" Owen asked.

"No! Your new pets *are* the gremlins," their dad replied.

"Surprise!" their mom added weakly.

A plate flew across the room and hit Owen in the head.

"Hehehehehehehehe!" the gremlin who'd thrown it laughed.

"Maybe next time we should just get them three-eyed goldenfish," Ella and Owen's dad whispered to their mom.

"**S**teeka stakka stakka sooo!" one gremlin said.

She grabbed a wooden stick and whacked Owen on the foot.

Owen's claws curled. "Tails and snails!" he grabbed his hurt foot and hopped around the house on his other one. "That really hurt!"

"It could be worse," Ella told him.

"How much worse?" Owen asked.

The gremlin hit Owen's other foot. "Tails and snails again!" Owen yelped. He grabbed his other foot and fell backward onto the ground.

"*That* much worse."

No wonder Ella and Owen's parents had heaved a huge sigh of relief upon their children's return and promptly gone to run errands, leaving their bat-squid dinners untouched and the gremlins in the twins' care.

Ella held her hand out to the gremlin with the stick. "Here you go. Hand it over. Come to Ella."

The gremlin laughed and ran out of the kitchen and toward Owen's bedroom.

"I'm gonna name my gremlin Owen Jr.," Owen said, looking at the other gremlin. "Come here, Owen Jr. Come on now."

KA-BONG! The gremlin threw a cooking pot, hitting Owen right in his snout.

"Hehehehehehehehehehe!" the gremlin laughed.

"Okay, maybe I won't call you Owen Jr.," Owen sighed. He pulled the pot from his snout.

"I like his laugh. You should call him Squeaky," Ella said.

KA-BONG! This time, Squeaky hit Owen with a frying pan.

"Why'd you throw it at me?" Owen pointed to his sister. "She's the one who named you Squeaky!"

Ella's gremlin ran from Owen's bedroom and back into the kitchen, carrying a book. The gremlin tore a page from it and ate it.

Owen screamed. "Aw, dragon scales! She's got one of my books!" He picked up the gremlin's stick. "Here, girl! Go get the stick! Fetch the stick!" Owen tossed it out the window.

"Fetta feeta feeta doooo," Ella's gremlin said as she dropped the book and took off after the stick, jumping out the window.

Owen ran to pick up his book. "Maybe these little guys can be trained after all," Owen said hopefully.

Ella's gremlin returned with the stick. She waved it around proudly before whacking Owen on the foot.

"OWW!!!" Owen dropped the book.

Squeaky picked up the book and threw it out the window.

Ella's gremlin picked up a stack of plates and started juggling them. But since gremlins don't know how to juggle, the plates kept breaking when they hit the ceiling.

"I've got the perfect name for mine," Ella said. "Nightmare."

3

THE GOOFY GREMLINS

Ella and Owen crept out from behind the kitchen table, where they had ducked for cover when Nightmare had begun throwing the plates instead of juggling them. Ella and Owen moved silently across the living room. Owen peeked out the front door as it suddenly got quiet.

"I don't see them anywhere," Owen said. "Do you?" Ella peeked out from behind their sofa.

"Nope," Ella replied. "I think we're gremlin free for now."

"That could be good. And it could be bad," Owen said. "What do you think they're up to?"

Just then Squeaky and Nightmare ran past Ella and Owen. Squeaky was holding a big straw hat and waving it in the air. "Hatta hedda hedda ping!" he yelled.

"I don't want to know," Ella said. "But I have a plan."

"If the rest of that sentence is 'to get rid of the gremlins,' then count me in," Owen said.

"We'll just return the gremlins to the pet store," Ella explained.

"I like the way you're thinking," Owen agreed. "How do we do that?"

"All we have to do is capture them first," Ella said.

"Okay, now that's the part I don't think I like," Owen said with a sigh.

"Don't worry," Ella said. "We just need a net." Ella reached for their father's fishing net by the front door. "Follow me."

The two dragons followed a trail
of destruction across their front yard
and through the woods to a clearing.

Nightmare and Squeaky sat around the
straw hat on the ground, squeaking
at it. Squeaky hit the hat with a stick.
"Hehehehehehehehe!" he squeaked.

Nightmare picked up the hat and put it on her head. She pulled it down so tightly that her head popped through the top.

Squeaky and Nightmare fell to the ground, laughing.

Ella and Owen crept on their tippy claws closer to the gremlins and hid behind a large rock.

"All we have to do is throw the net over them and wrap them up," Ella whispered.

"Oh, is *that* all?" Owen whispered sarcastically. "I thought we were going to do something impossible."

The dragons leaped from behind the rock with the net.

The startled gremlins jumped into the air in fright.

Nightmare tore off the hat and threw it at Owen's feet.

"Gremlin hat attack!" yelled Owen. He tripped over the hat and plopped to the ground, letting go of the net.

Ella tripped over Owen and rolled across the dirt. The net rolled with her, wrapping Owen's wings tightly against her body. They rolled to the edge of a cliff and stopped.

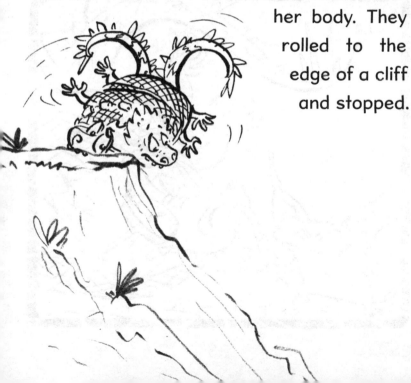

"Whew!" Owen said. "That was close."

"Don't move," Ella said, peeking over the edge. "Don't even breathe. It's a long way down."

Squeaky ran over to the dragons and tickled Owen's nose with a feather. "Teeeka takka takka taak," he said.

"Don't you dare sneeze," Ella warned.

"I can't—I can't—ACHOOOO!" Fire shot from Owen's snout and sent the dragons bouncing down the hill.

"OUCH! OUCH!" Ella shrieked.

The dragons rolled to a stop at the bottom.

A pile of gross slugs splatted onto their heads.

Owen wiggled free of the net and wiped the slugs off his face.

Nightmare and Squeaky raced away carrying an empty bucket.

"Yukka yook yook yeh!" Squeaky happily yelled out.

"I wish Mom and Dad got us a couple of three-horned moon moths instead," Ella said. "At least they're quiet and don't make a mess."

"I have an idea," Owen said.

"Oh, great. Does it involve me falling down a hill again?" Ella complained.

"No," Owen replied. "I once read that the best way to catch a gremlin is to make it go to sleep."

"What if they *never* fall asleep?" Ella asked, picking a gross slug from her scales. "What if they stay awake forever?!"

"Well, then that would be very bad," Owen said.

"You know what *else* would be very bad?" Ella asked. "If they had friends!"

"That's crazy!" Owen laughed. "Who'd want to be friends with a gremlin?!"

"MORE GREMLINS!" Ella screamed, pointing behind her brother.

In the distance, Nightmare and Squeaky were running from the woods with two more gremlins.

"Squeeeka peeka peeka fooo!" Squeaky babbled.

The other gremlins grabbed handfuls of pop-pop berries and threw them down at Ella and Owen.

The pop-pop berries exploded, covering the two dragons in sticky, orange pop-pop berry juice.

"Do you know what I'm thinking?" Owen asked.

"That an all-gremlin playdate is a terrible idea?" Ella answered.

"It's the *most* terrible, awful, no-good idea ever!" Owen grumbled.

The four gremlins raced back into the woods, squealing with delight.

"At least someone's having a good time with our new pets," Owen said.

"Yeah. It's just too bad it's not us," Ella growled.

OWEN'S AWESOME GREMLIN TRAP!

"Are you sure this is gonna work?" Ella scratched her scaly head with a claw.

Ella and Owen had needed over an hour to wash all the sticky pop-pop berry juice from their scales. The dragon twins could handle the gremlins smashing their plates and even messing up their home,

but making them both take a bath—that was the last straw!

"You bet your tail it will work. You may not know it, but dragons are experts at building gremlin traps," Owen replied.

"You're right. I didn't know that," Ella replied. "And I'm a dragon!"

"It's one of our twenty-seven dragon skills," Owen explained.

"Twenty-seven dragon skills? I never heard of those before, and, once again, I'm a dragon!" Ella said.

"Then I guess *you* have only twenty-*six* dragon skills," Owen replied.

"Sometimes I think you have a few too many loose scales on your noggin." Ella shook her head. "Now, how does this trap work?"

"Well, first the gremlins walk into the trap."

Owen pointed to a spring attached to a block of wood. "And then this spring sproings," he said.

He pointed to a rope that hung from a tree branch. Owen had tied a log at the end of the rope.

"Then that makes the log doodad swing down and hit that thingy there."

He pointed to a pole stuck in the ground. A ball was balanced on top of it.

"Then the pole thing falls over, and that ball thingamajig bounces across the whatchamacallit."

He tapped the side of a slide. "The ball thing then rolls onto the thingamajig."

Owen pointed to a rope that was attached to the bottom of the slide. The other end of the rope hung from a tall tree and was attached to a bamboo cage. "And *that* makes the cage fall, trapping them. Then we take them back to the pet store."

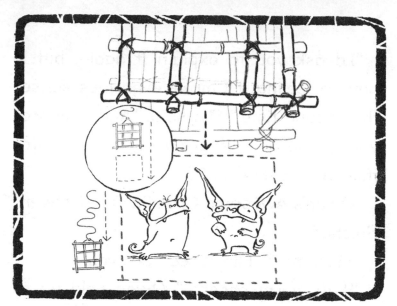

Owen put his hands on his hips and stood proudly in front of his creation.

"I'd ask you to explain it again, but I have a feeling it'll make even less sense the second time," Ella said. "And how are you gonna get the gremlins to walk into this, um . . . this . . . ?"

"Owen's Awesome Gremlin Trap," Owen finished.

"Yeah, *that*." Ella rolled her eyes.

"With worm cheese!" Owen held up a piece of foul-smelling cheese with worms in it. "Gremlins love it because it gives them bad breath."

"Ugh! Gremlin breath is worse than ogre burps." Ella pinched her nose.

Owen was about to place the worm cheese onto the spring platform when Squeaky swung past on a vine and snatched up the worm cheese from Owen's claws.

"Hahahahahahaha!" the gremlin laughed.

"Aw, dragon scales! We need to get him before he eats the worm cheese! That was my only piece!" Owen shouted. Squeaky swung from tree branch to tree branch.

The twin dragons tried to trap the gremlin by flying at him from opposite directions, but Squeaky ducked at the last second.

BONK!

Ella and Owen crashed into each other.

"Hehehehehehehehe!" Squeaky laughed and ran back to the trap. He placed the worm cheese on the spring platform and raced away.

"Quick! Grab the worm cheese before he comes back and takes it away again!" Owen said.

Ella and Owen raced to the gremlin trap and grabbed the worm cheese from the spring platform.

"Who's the smart one now, gremlin?!" Owen laughed.

Without the weight of the cheese holding it down, the spring platform sprung up.

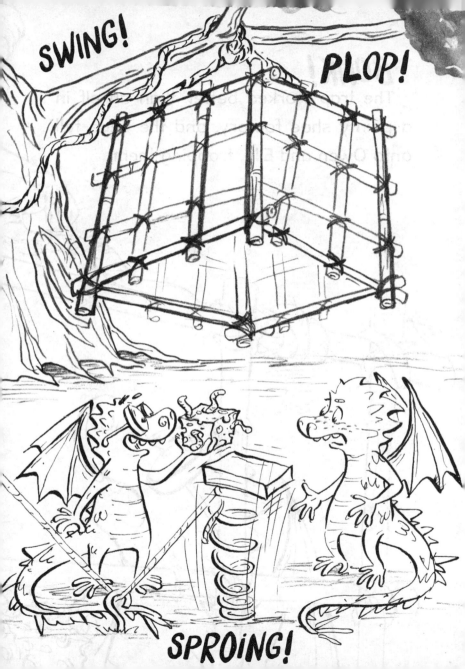

BONK!

The trap worked better than an elf in a pointy shoe factory, and the cage fell onto Owen and Ella, trapping them.

"So, uh, the answer to your question of 'Who's the smart one now,'" Ella began. ". . . I'd have to say . . . it's not us."

"**W**ell, this could've gone much better," Ella said with a sigh.

"At least it didn't go *worse*," Owen said.

Those six words had barely left Owen's mouth when the four gremlins jumped to the branches overhead and poured a bucket of gross slugs down on the dragons.

"Okay, now it's worse," Owen sighed.

"Dragon tails! This is the third time I'll have to clean my scales today!" Ella complained. "And I hate baths!"

"Ella! Owen! Just the dragons we were looking for!" called out Sparkle Pop the unicorn as she trotted down the path toward them with her twin, Glitter Star.

"We were just traveling from the Lollipop Forest to visit you guys," Glitter Star said. "But we didn't think you two lived in a cage."

"We don't. Our new pets trapped us," Ella explained.

"What kind of pets trap their owners in a cage?" Glitter Star asked.

Those ten words had barely left Glitter Star's mouth when the four gremlins poured gross slugs onto the two unicorns from the treetops above.

"Gremlins!!!" Ella and Owen said together.

"But you gotta wonder. Where do they keep finding all these gross slugs?" Owen asked.

The two unicorns cleaned off the slugs, and then Sparkle Pop used the point of his horn to open the cage door's lock. Ella and Owen flew out, happier than witches in a Nothing but Turnips store.

"Are you guys here to give us more unicorn rides?" Owen asked hopefully.

"Or better yet . . . can you help us catch these gremlins and return them to the pet shop?" Ella asked.

"You-nicorn betcha! The best way to catch a gremlin is to make it fall asleep," Sparkle Pop said.

"We know," Ella said.

"But whatever you do, *don't* let them bring their friends over!" Sparkle Pop warned.

"We know!" Ella said.

"It's lucky we came to visit because rubbing a gremlin with a unicorn mane will make it fall asleep instantly," Glitter Star said and flopped his thick mane to one side.

"Why does that work?" Owen asked.

"Because unicorns are awesome," Glitter Star said with a loud neigh. "And I've got the best mane in all the seven Candy Cane Kingdoms!"

"Uh, nice try, bro," Sparkle Pop said. "But no one has a better mane than I do!" Sparkle Pop let her long mane wave in the breeze.

"Your mane looks like an ogre's mustache!" Glitter Star laughed.

"And yours looks like a centaur's tail!" Sparkle Pop sneered.

"I've seen nicer hair on a troll's toes!" Glitter Star said.

"And I've seen nicer hair in a troll's *nose*!" Sparkle Pop replied.

"You *both* have manes nicer than a troll's armpit or whatever, so don't worry," Owen said.

Glitter Star and Sparkle Pop glared at Owen.

"Ignore my brother. He has beetles for brains," Ella said. "You both have awesome manes. Now can we please get rid of these gremlins before they invite over more gremlin friends?"

"It's too late!" Owen yelped. "Look!"

The dragons and unicorns turned to see Nightmare creeping from the forest with more friends.

Many, *many* more friends.

"Meena matta mook mook maaaaa!" Nightmare laughed.

"What does that mean?" Sparkle Pop asked.

"I don't know, but I've got a bad feeling we're about to find out," Ella replied.

"Look out!" Owen yelled.

"Duck!" Ella warned.

"Run away!" Glitter Star called out.

"Hide!" Sparkle Pop shouted.

Troll belly button moss flew through the air. Terror Swamp sludge balls splattered the ground. Crusty ogre toenail grime poured down from the trees overhead. Ella, Owen, Sparkle Pop, and Glitter Star ran around in a panic, trying to avoid the gunk the laughing gremlins were throwing at them from all directions.

"At least they ran out of gross slugs!" Owen said, ducking under a snail slime spitball Nightmare flung at him.

SPLASH!

A bucket full of gross slugs tumbled onto Owen's head.

"Aw, dragon scales!" Owen said as gross slugs squirmed across his wings. "They get me with that every time."

"Hehehehehehehehe!" Squeaky laughed. He threw more slugs at Ella, then picked up two more handfuls and slopped them onto his own head, shouting out, "Meee moppa moppa mop!"

Nightmare and the other gremlins laughed crazily. "Moppa moppa mop!" they shouted and dumped buckets of slugs onto their own heads as well.

"In case there was any doubt left, gremlins are crazy," Owen said.

"Hahahahahahaha!" Nightmare laughed, then called out, "Peeta paaata beeta boo!" to the other gremlins.

"I am not sticking around to see if 'Peeta paaata beeta boo' is worse than 'Meena matta mook mook maaaaa' 'cause that was pretty bad!" Owen said.

Owen and the others dove for cover behind a prickleberry bush, but there was no gremlin attack.

"Listen!" Ella said. "Do you hear that?"

"The only thing I hear is the sound of our doom!" Owen said.

"No . . . *listen*!" Ella said. "It's totally quiet."

"Except for the sound of our doom!" Owen whispered.

"Ella's right," Glitter Star said. He peeked out from the prickleberry bush. "It *is* quiet. The gremlins must be gone."

"Oh, no! I'm not falling for that!" Owen said. "The gremlins want us to *think* it's quiet because then we won't hear the sound of our doom, which sounds just like everything being quiet!"

"What do you think they're up to?" Sparkle Pop asked.

"Our doom," Owen added.

"I don't know, but it can't be good," Ella answered.

"Look out! Duck! Run away! Hide!" Voices shouted from just outside the forest.

"That's coming from Dragon Patch!" Ella said. "Come on!"

Owen, Ella, Sparkle Pop, and Glitter Star rushed to Dragon Patch and arrived in time to see a gnome race past them, yelling, "Doooooooom!"

"Why does no one ever listen to me?" Owen huffed.

Dragon Patch was a disaster! Gremlins were everywhere! They swung from the statue of Dragon Patch's founder, Orblag the Emerald Dragon. They swung from dwarves' beards. They even swung from the sign that said NO SWINGING!

They played on the heads of angry
ogres like bongos, made the trolls take
baths, and shook all the pixie dust from
the pockets of panicked pixies. They even
ordered pointy shoes from Evelyn Elf's
Pointy Shoe Palace without saying please
or thank you.

"This is all *your* fault!" Ken the grumpy wizard pointed a finger at Ella and Owen.

"Huh? Why do you think this is our fault?" Owen asked.

"Because *everything* is your fault! *Always!*" Ken answered. "And even when it's *not* your fault, it's still your fault! Somehow." Ken's face grew red with anger. "Look what these little beasts did! They took my favorite wizard hat!" Ken motioned to his hatless head. "What kind of wizard doesn't have a pointy hat?!"

"A grumpy one?" Ella answered.

"Um . . . I think they may have taken something much worse than your hat," Owen said nervously.

"Nothing's worse than taking a wizard's hat!" Ken growled.

"Oh, I can think of one thing a lot worse," Owen said, pointing to Nightmare, who was riding on the shoulders of another gremlin and waving Ken's magic wand in the air.

"Okay, so that is a lot worse," Ken said and ran behind a tree for cover. "If my wand glows with purple magical energy, that spell's gonna be a doozy!"

The tip of Ken's wand glowed a deeper and deeper purple.

"It's been nice knowing you, Sis." Owen's wings nervously knocked together.

"Please don't turn us into trolls!" Glitter Star whimpered. "I don't wanna smell like moldy dwarf shoes!"

"Hahahahahahaha!" Nightmare laughed and pointed the glowing wand at Ella.

Ella squinted her dragon eyes, wrinkled her nose, and shouted, "FREE UNICORN RIDES!"

"WHAT?!" Sparkle Pop and Glitter Star shouted together.

"Me first!" Owen called out and hopped up onto Glitter Star's back.

Nightmare dropped the magic wand. He and the other gremlins shouted happy nonsense and piled onto the backs of Glitter Star and Sparkle Pop, knocking Owen off so they could get a ride.

"Hey! No cuts-ies!" Owen whined.

And then, as quickly as the madcap chaos had started, it ended as all the gremlins fell asleep the moment they brushed up against Glitter Star's and Sparkle Pop's manes.

THUD! THUD! THUD!

The gremlins dropped to the ground like rotten apples falling from a tree, happily snoring in deep sleep.

"You can thank me now," Ella said with a smile.

"Whoa! Great idea, Ella!" Sparkle Pop cheered.

"And the best part is, now *I* get a unicorn ride!" Owen said and jumped back onto Glitter Star's back.

Ella, Owen, Sparkle Pop, and Glitter Star brought the sleeping gremlins back to the pet shop. They were surprised that it only took thirty minutes of begging, two pop-pop berry pies, four unicorn rides, one dragon ride, and a small box of ogre wart remover to convince the pet shop owner to take the gremlins—and their friends—back.

"Twelve . . . thirteen . . . fourteen . . ."
Owen counted the gremlins as they put
them in the gremlin cage. "How many
were there again?"

"More than one, and that's one too
many!" Ella slammed the cage door shut.

"Are you sure Nightmare and Squeaky are *both* in there?" Owen asked. "It's really hard to tell. They all kinda look alike. . . ."

"Squeaky is the annoying one and Nightmare is the annoying and mean one," Ella said.

"I'm so glad that's over!" Glitter Star sighed. "Now we can all go do something fun like—"

The foursome turned to leave, but muddy elves, clean trolls, dwarves with half their beards shaved off, pixie-dust-covered pixies, and one wizard without his wand and his favorite pointy wizard hat were blocking the pet shop's doorway. They all glared angrily at Ella and Owen.

". . . Like clean up the big mess those no-good gremlins made?" Ella said meekly. "Right? Ha ha. That sure sounds 'fun.'"

Ella, Owen, and the two unicorns spent the rest of the day cleaning, fixing, sweeping, and making trolls smelly again by rubbing old gross slugs on their backs. They even found Ken's favorite wizard hat jammed into a dwarf's beard.

"I'm so tired, even my horn fell asleep," Sparkle Pop moaned once they finished cleaning up the gremlins' mayhem.

"I'm even too tired to be majestic," Glitter Star said, unable to muster up even a slightly heroic pose.

"Thanks for your help," Ella yawned. "I'm gonna go curl up and sleep for the next hundred years."

"Maybe next time you can come visit *us*," Glitter Star said. "The only thing we have to worry about in the Lollipop Forest is getting cavities."

The four friends said their goodbyes and headed home.

Owen's wings sagged and his tail dragged as he and Ella trudged into their bedrooms for some much-needed sleep.

"**AAAAAAAAH!**" Ella screamed.
"**AAAAAAAAH!**" Owen screamed.

"*AAAAAAH!*" Squeaky screamed.

Squeaky the gremlin was on Owen's bed, jumping up and down on a book.

"We must have missed Squeaky!" Ella said.

Squeaky grabbed the book and raced from the house. "Hehehehehehehe!" he giggled.

"Let's pretend we never saw him and hope we never see him again," Ella said.

"We have to go after him!" Owen gasped. "He's got my favorite book, *The Adventures of Azerath the Blue Dragon*!"

"It's just a *book*!" Ella replied.

"It. Is. Not. Just. A Book!" Owen huffed. "IT'S AZERATH!" He flew after Squeaky.

"Ah well, this'll probably be more fun than sleeping!" Ella flapped her wings and quickly zoomed after her brother.

Read on for a sneak peek from the ninth book in
the Ella and Owen series, *Grumpy Goblins*

ELLA AND OWEN

GRUMPY GOBLINS

by Jaden Kent

illustrated by Iryna Bodnaruk

"**H**e went this way! Come on!" Owen yelled to his twin sister Ella as the two dragons flew through the woods after their new pet gremlin, Squeaky.

Well, it wasn't exactly their new pet. Ella and Owen's parents had gotten them a surprise gift—two gremlins that turned into a lot of gremlins when their gremlin friends showed up and nearly destroyed the dragons' home. Ella and Owen had managed to catch and return all the gremlins to the pet shop. Except for Squeaky, who had somehow gotten loose and taken Owen's favorite book with him.

Ella and Owen chased Squeaky through the forest, following his footprints in the soft, muddy ground.

"Yup, he surely went this way," Owen said.

"Can we please just forget the book and go home? I'm so tired of chasing gremlins!" Ella pleaded.

She looked over her shoulder. Their home in Dragon Patch was getting farther away with every wing flap. "If we fly much farther ahead, I'll never get back in time for the Dragon Games. How am I supposed to win the Winged Wonders Flying Championship if I'm not even there?"

"Don't worry, Squeaky's got to be just ahead of us," Owen said. "I can smell the stink of his stinky gremlin feet even from up here. We'll make it in time for your silly Dragon Games."

"I've been training for a year so I can compete!" Ella said. "I will not miss them because of some silly book."

"It's not 'some silly' book! It's my absolute favorite book!" Owen said. "*The Adventures of Azerath the Blue Dragon*!"

"But gremlins can't even read!" Ella shouted.

"Their loss!" Owen exclaimed. "It's the best book ever! Azerath flies to the edge of the world and he has to battle the Dark Troll to save the kingdom of—"

"SNORE!" Ella pretended to doze off to interrupt Owen's explanation.

"Fine. See if I invite you to Azerath-Con next month," Owen said with a huff. "And I'm a guest of honor!" He flew off to find Squeaky.

Ella sighed and followed him. "Probably

the only guest," she said under her breath.

Owen folded his wings in and swiftly landed behind a tree.

"The footprints stop here. . . ." he said, concerned.

"Oh well, we lost him!" Ella said, not concerned. "Time to go home, I guess!"

THUD!

THUD!

THUD!

"Did you hear that?" Owen asked.

"No! I did not hear anything that sounded like an annoying gremlin jumping up and down on your favorite book!" Ella answered.

"Hold on, Azerath! I'm coming to save you!" Owen called out and raced toward the noise.